THIS BLOOMSBURY BOOK

BELONGS TO

....

*For Stuart who showed me the colours, and
Stuart J, Graeme and Cara, who keep them
bright - LS*

*To Joe
Lots of love from Great Uncle David! - DW*

**BLOOMSBURY
CHILDREN'S
BOOKS**

Published by Bloomsbury, New York and London
Distributed to the trade by Holtzbrinck Publishers

Library of Congress Cataloging-in-Publication Data available upon request

First U.S. Edition 2003

Printed in China

1 3 5 7 9 10 8 6 4 2

Bloomsbury USA Children's Books
175 Fifth Avenue
New York, New York 10010

What Color is Love?

BLOOMSBURY
CHILDREN'S
BOOKS

by Linda Strachan
illustrated by David Wojtowycz

"What color is love?"

asked Small Smooth and Gray.

"Could it be green?"

Said old wrinkly Grandpa,

"I don't know if that's true,

but grass is green –
so love might be blue."

"What color is love?"

asked Small Smooth and Gray.

"Could it be blue?"

Tiger turned over
and rolled on his back.

"I can't tell you the answer,
my little fellow,

the sky is blue –
maybe love could be yellow?"

"What color is love?"
asked Small Smooth and Gray.

"Could it be yellow?"

Lion opened an eye, too tired to play.

He yawned and he said,
"This hot sun is yellow –
isn't love red?"

Parrot looked down
from his perch in the tree.

"Red is for flowers, but love is so bright,
it's really quite simple – love must be white!"

"What
color
is love?"

asked
Small Smooth and Gray.

"Could it be white?"

"No,
love isn't
white,"

said Zebra.

"No, I think ...
love is so wonderful –
it must be pink!"

"No, that can't be right.
Love should be orange
        like the sunset at night."

Tired and exhausted
at the end of the day,
"I know who to ask,"
said Small Smooth and Gray.

He left Flamingo
    with his tall slender legs,

and passed by Zebra
    on the old river bed.

Lion had gone from his rock in the sun.

and Tiger, out hunting,
set off at a run.

He went to the water and dipped in his toe.
He said to his mother, "Does nobody know?
I've tried all the colors, from the grass to the flowers,
from the sky, to the clouds,
to the sun up above ...

but no one could tell me
the color of
love."

"What color is love?
I'll tell you little one ...

It's as dark
as the night

and as bright
as the sun.

Imagine a color
and love is right there,

love is every color,
    everything,
        everywhere.

"What color is love?
Every color,

all around ...
... because nothing
else matters

when it's Love that
you've found."

Enjoy more great picture books from Bloomsbury Children's Books ...

Goodnight Lulu
Paulette Bogan

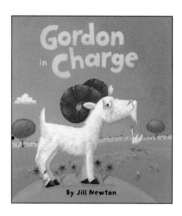

Gordon in Charge
Jill Newton

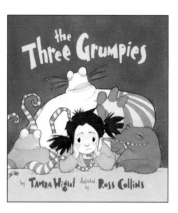

The Three Grumpies
Tamra Wight & Ross Collins

Hector the Hermit Crab
Katie Boyce

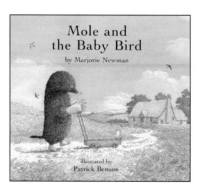

Mole and the Baby Bird
Marjorie Newman & Patrick Benson